A Note to Parents and Caregivers:

Read-it! Joke Books are for children who are moving ahead on the amazing road to reading. These fun books support the acquisition and extension of reading skills as well as a love of books.

Published by the same company that produces *Read-it!* Readers, these books introduce the question/answer and dialogue patterns that help children expand their thinking about language structure and book formats.

When sharing joke books with a child, read in short stretches. Pause often to talk about the pictures and the meaning of the jokes. The question/answer and dialogue formats work well for this purpose. Have the child turn the pages and point to the pictures and familiar words. When you read the jokes, have fun creating the voices of characters or emphasizing some important words. And be sure to reread favorite jokes.

There is no right or wrong way to share books with children. Find time to read with your child, and pass on the legacy of literacy.

Adria F. Klein, Ph.D.
Professor Emeritus
California State University
San Bernardino, California

Managing Editor: Bob Temple
Creative Director: Terri Foley
Editor: Peggy Henrikson
Editorial Adviser: Andrea Cascardi
Designer: Amy Muehlenhardt
Page production: Picture Window Books
The illustrations in this book were prepared digitally.

Picture Window Books
5115 Excelsior Boulevard
Suite 232
Minneapolis, MN 55416
1-877-845-8392
www.picturewindowbooks.com

Printed in the United States of America.

Library of Congress Cataloging-in-Publication Data
Dahl, Michael.
Family funnies / written by Michael Dahl ; illustrated by Ryan Haugen.
p. cm. — (Read-it! joke books)
Summary: A collection of jokes and riddles about members of the family.
ISBN 1-4048-0304-1
1. Family—Juvenile humor. 2. Wit and humor, Juvenile. [1. Family—Wit
and humor. 2. Jokes. 3. Riddles.] I. Haugen, Ryan, ill. II. Title.
PN6231.F3 D34 2004
815'.5402—dc22
                                                              2003016662

Family Funnies

A Book of Family Jokes

Michael Dahl • Illustrated by Ryan Haugen

Reading Advisers:
Adria F. Klein, Ph.D.
Professor Emeritus, California State University
San Bernardino, California

Susan Kesselring, M.A., Literacy Educator
Rosemount-Apple Valley-Eagan (Minnesota) School District

PICTURE WINDOW BOOKS
Minneapolis, Minnesota

Mom: "Why did you put a frog in your brother's bed?"

Joey: "Because I
couldn't find a snake."

When do mothers have baby boys?

OCTOBER

Sunday	Monday	Tuesday	Wednesday	Thursday
		1	2	3
		8	9	
	7			
14				

On Son Days.

Billy: "We got a dog for
our little sister."

Sam: "I wish my dad would let *me*
make a trade like that."

Tommy: "Why? Is one missing?"

Where do little monkeys live?

In the family tree.

Amy: "Why is your sister so small?"

Matt: "She's my half sister."

Second monster: "Did they keep him?"

Dad: "Don't be selfish.
Share your new bicycle with
your little brother."

Mike: "I do. I use it going down the hill, and he gets to use it going up." 17

Teacher: "Do you like to share things, Sarah?"
Sarah: "Yes, I do."
Teacher: "What's something you share with your brother?"

Sarah: "Our parents."

Mom: "Sammy, please stop pulling my hair!"

Sammy: "I want my gum back!"

Ben: "My gramma is visiting us for the holidays."
Tammy: "Where does your gramma live?"

Ben: "At the airport. Whenever we want her, we just go out there and get her."

What do Abominable Snowmothers have?

Chill-dren.

Who is married to Antarctica?

Uncle Arctica.